For the pupils and staff of Broomhill Primary School, Glasgow

Published by Sunbird Books, an imprint of Phoenix International Publications, Inc.

8501 West Higgins Road   59 Gloucester Place
Chicago, Illinois 60631   London W1U 8JJ

www.sunbirdkidsbooks.com

Text and illustrations © 2021 Sally Anne Garland

Sunbird Books and the colophon are trademarks of Phoenix International Publications, Inc.

Library of Congress Control Number: 2020947772

ISBN: 978-1-5037-5848-3   Printed in China

The art for this book was created with pencil and paper and the aid of a computer.
Text set in IM FELL Double Pica.

NOOK

Written and illustrated by Sally Anne Garland

sunbird books

Nook was small
and gentle, and she
rarely spoke.

She liked to sit in quiet places, with her back pressed firmly against something so that she felt safe.

She would wedge into corners...

...and squeeze into boxes.

She would press
against walls,
and squish tight into
big, comfy chairs.

So it was no surprise that her favorite place outside was the low, deep hollow of an old elm tree.

The hollow was perfect. Nook could watch the others play but still feel safe, pressed against the back of the tree.

From time to time, the others
would try to coax her out.

Nook always stayed put...
but her spirit followed
the others when they
went back to play.

The hollow soon became
known as "Nook's place,"
and the others would know
not to sit there.

But one day that changed.

"Mine!"
an angry face snapped.
"Go away!"

Poor Nook. She didn't know what to do.
She could feel her panic rise and the
hot tears of her silence well up as
she stood trembling, with nothing
at her back to protect her.

Suddenly, she heard a
voice behind her.
"That's Nook's place,"
the voice said.

"Yes, Nook needs
to sit there," said
another voice.

To Nook's surprise, the others were standing right behind her, and now they stepped closer to make her feel safe.

"It's mine!" snapped the angry
face once again.

But the others simply said,
"Come on Nook, you're with
us," and Nook, feeling braver,
followed them to the middle
of the playground.

The hollow was empty the next day,
and the next, and the next...
but Nook chose not to sit there.

Instead, she played quietly
in the middle with her friends,
who she knew had her back.